∤
W171mk

MARIAH KEEPS COOL

by Mildred Pitts Walter

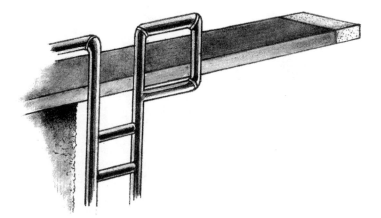

Bradbury Press   New York

The text of this book is set in 14 point Caledonia.
The illustrations are pencil drawings reproduced as halftones.
Typography by Julie Quan

Bradbury Press
An Affiliate of Macmillan, Inc.
866 Third Avenue, New York, NY 10022
Collier Macmillan Canada, Inc.

Printed and bound in the United States of America
First Edition
10 9 8 7 6 5 4 3 2 1

LIBRARY OF CONGRESS CATALOGING-IN-PUBLICATION DATA
Walter, Mildred Pitts.
Mariah keeps cool / Mildred Pitts Walter. — 1st ed.
p.   cm.
Summary: Eleven-year-old Mariah envisions a great summer
competing as a diver and planning a surprise party for her sister
Lynn but half sister Denise proves a cloud in Mariah's
sunny summer.
ISBN 0-02-792295-2
[1. Family life—Fiction.   2. Sisters—Fiction.   3. Afro
-Americans—Fiction.]   I. Title.
PZ7.W17125Mao   1990
[Fic]—dc20   89-23981   CIP   AC

To all young people who find joy
in the pursuit of excellence

They had hardly gotten into the house from the airport. Even before Denise unpacked her bags, Mariah wanted to call her friends, the Friendly Five. They must rush over and meet her new sister.

"Now, Mariah," Mama said, "calm down. Give us time to get acquainted."

"Yeah, let Denise at least unpack," Lynn pleaded.

Somewhat thwarted, Mariah still let her spirit soar. She rushed ahead of them to the room prepared for Denise, threw open the door, and shouted, "Welcome! Hope you like this room."

1

Denise didn't say yes, and she didn't say no. She unpacked a small bag that held gifts: a pair of earrings for Mama, a pen that held real ink for Daddy, and a package for Lynn. When Lynn unwrapped a book, Mariah cried, "Look at that! First you give me a Sheik Bashara poster at the airport, and now you give Lynn a book. How'd you know what we'd like?"

"We have the same daddy, you know," Denise said, and grinned.

Mariah looked at Mama, remembering the uneasiness they had felt about Daddy bringing the child of another marriage to live in their home.

A surge of joy rushed through Mariah as she and Lynn helped Denise unpack. Right away she saw that Denise didn't wear clothes from resale shops. That Denise's clothes were more like hers than Lynn's made Mariah especially happy. As they put things in the closet and into drawers, she did all the talking. Did Denise really like the room? How long would she stay? What was Denise's mama like? Did she want to—

"Please Mariah," Lynn interrupted, "stop talking so much and put these things away." She handed Mariah suitcases. Lynn's tone made Mariah aware that Denise was not as eager to answer questions as she was to ask them.

With the unpacking done, Lynn went to help Mama finish dinner while Mariah insisted that Denise see the rest of the house. She showed her own room last.

"Wow!" Denise exclaimed when she walked into Mariah's room. "You're not a Sheik fan; you're a Sheik fanatic."

"Oooo, I just love him." Mariah rushed to display her records and pamphlets, the Sheik earrings and shoestrings, and the aluminum wall hanging. When she showed Denise the program from the Sheik concert she sighed, "Aahh. I was there and you know what? He kissed my hand."

"I just bet he did," Denise said, not believing a word.

"Cross my heart and hope to die."

"Really?"

"Really! Now help me find just the right place for my new poster."

"That's gonna take genius thinking."

Before they got started, Lynn called to say it was time for dinner.

"Just a minute, Lynn. We're busy."

"We'll have plenty of time," Denise promised, putting her arm around Mariah's shoulder. "I'll be here awhile." Mariah felt happy as she and Denise went to join the rest of the family for dinner.

Daddy had Denise sit beside Lynn, who was across the table from Mariah. That pleased Mariah. She still had her place next to Daddy, who sat at the head of the table.

"Now we're five. Hey, Denise, my best friends and I call ourselves the Friendly Five. You just got to meet them. When can they come over, Mama?"

"You have plenty of time, Mariah. Maybe tomorrow."

"My friend Kim is having a party tomorrow night," Lynn said. "Would you like to come, Denise?"

"You didn't tell me Kim was having a party," Mariah complained. "Can I go?"

"If you had been invited, I would have told you. No, you can't go," Lynn replied.

"Mama, tell her to let me go," Mariah pleaded.

"It's Kim's party and you're not invited," Mama answered. "Denise, I think you'll like Kim."

"Am I invited?" Denise wanted to know.

"Oh, sure. I'll call Kim," Lynn assured Denise.

Mariah, stung by Lynn's refusal to ask Kim to invite her, became quiet. She should be able to go. After all, she was now eleven years old, she thought. She listened to Denise and their daddy talk about people they had known when Denise lived with their grandma, Daddy's mother, before Denise went away to live with her mother in another town.

"Daddy, remember Tracy?" Denise asked. "When I lived here she was my best friend in the third grade. Tracy Woods."

"Tracy Woods. *Your* best friend?" Mariah blurted out. "She's not a very nice girl."

"Riah! You don't ever think before you open your mouth. You don't even know Tracy," Lynn scolded.

6

"Who doesn't know Tracy? We all know she's a dropout."

"Enough, Mariah," Daddy said. Then he turned to Denise and said, "Tracy is still here. We don't see her, though."

When they had cleared the table and were about to do dishes, Denise volunteered to help.

"No, it's my week to do the dishes," Mariah said.

"They take turns, Denise," Mama explained. "One week one does the dishes while the other helps prepare the food. Can you cook?"

"Goodness, no. My mama and I eat out a lot: fried chicken, mashed potatoes and gravy, hamburgers and fries. I don't cook," Denise said unashamedly.

"Lynn is a good cook," Daddy said.

"And what about me?" Mariah wanted to know.

"Well, you're getting there," Mama said, and they all laughed, except Mariah.

7

Later that evening, when Mariah went to bed, she still felt the sting of Lynn inviting Denise and not her to Kim's party. And they had the nerve to laugh at my cooking. In front of Denise. What gives with Denise? Mariah wondered. Still, she was pleased that she had already learned a little bit about her new sister. She knew she had a lot more to learn.

The day had been exciting and she felt tired, but there was still a moment for Sheik. She took the small picture of Sheik from the table near her bed and kissed his lips. She held the picture to her heart.

"Good night, my love," she whispered. Then she replaced the picture and snuggled down to a satisfying sleep.

The next day Mariah was so excited she could hardly wait for her friends to come. Just as she and Denise finished hanging the new poster near her mirror, the doorbell rang. Her friends had arrived, all at the same time.

Cynthia, Jerri, Nikki, and Trina crowded into Mariah's room. "Look!" Mariah pointed at the new poster. There were shrieks of delight.

"Where'd you find *that*?" Jerri screamed.

"Oooo, love it," Trina shouted. "I've gotta have one just like it."

"Wait, wait, now," Mariah cried. "You got to meet my sister." She pulled them all together near her and said, "Denise, we are the Friendly Five." When she had finished the introduction, Mariah went on, "It's a neat poster, huh? *She* gave it to me." Mariah threw her arms around Denise's waist.

"I thought so. You could never find anything boss like that here," Trina said.

"Oh there're neat things here, too, huh, Nikki?" Jerri asked.

"Don't ask me." Nikki flopped on Mariah's bed.

As soon as Denise had excused herself and left the room, they all started talking at once.

"Oh, she's cute," Trina said.

"You think she looks like Lynn?" Mariah wanted to know.

"Yeah," they all cried at once.

"And like your daddy," Cynthia said.

Mariah beamed. "She's blood and you

all are my best friends." They were quiet for a moment and Mariah felt sure they knew that she spoke the truth.

"Now that your sister is here, you'll probably put us down for the summer," Cynthia said.

"No way," Mariah promised. "I love you guys. And I just *love* summer." She went on, "The swimming pool opens today and there's an all-city swimming and diving meet coming up. We ought to get in it."

"We say that every summer, and we never do," Nikki said.

"We can't swim in a big meet like that," Trina said.

"We're good, fast swimmers," Jerri countered. "We could compete if we really worked hard."

"We should," Mariah suggested. "And if we do, let's ask Brandon to coach us." Brandon was a classmate.

"You really want Brandon? You know

how important he thinks he is," Trina said.

"He's a fantastic swimmer, girl. And you ought to see him dive," Jerri declared. "He went to swim camp three years in a row."

"He should be good, with that big pool he's got," Trina said. "And if we're gonna do it, we better get over to the rec center and sign up."

They made plans to sign up for the swim meet and to ask Brandon to coach them. Then they listened to Sheik Bashara records. By the time the girls left, Mariah felt assured that her summer was off to a good start.

Mariah and her friends left the recreation center excited about the swimming competition. Mr. Lyons, the swim director, told them they each must have a thorough physical examination before they would be permitted to train. He applauded their signing up, for though there were a lot of good swimmers there, the center had never participated in the all-city meet. He agreed to let Brandon assist him as their coach, but he wanted them to train as a team at the center. He would take responsibility for them at the meet.

Mariah had suggested that Brandon join them at Nikki's because Nikki lived closest to the center.

"We'd better hurry," Trina suggested. "You know that Brandon. If we're late he'll leave."

"I hope he'll coach us," Mariah said. "But we gotta make it easy for ourselves. There are five categories: diving, backstroke, breaststroke, butterfly, and freestyle. We should each take one and train for that."

"Good idea, Mariah," Jerri agreed.

"Yeah, that way we can win," Cynthia said.

"And we won't have to work so hard," Nikki said.

"You kidding? It's gonna be hard work no matter what," Jerri complained.

When they arrived at Nikki's, Brandon was just getting there, too.

"You better have a good reason for

getting me out of bed," Brandon called.

"What? We've been up for hours," Mariah bragged.

"Well, I don't want to be up even now, so this had better be important."

When they had settled in Nikki's backyard, they explained to Brandon what they wanted to do. "Will you be our coach?" Mariah asked.

"I don't know. It depends. . . ."

"On *what*, Brandon?" Trina demanded. "Don't be so negative."

"I'm interested, but only if you guys are serious. Swimming competition is hard work. I don't know how hard you want to work."

"Hard, Brandon," Mariah said. "Each one of us will do an event and do it well. We want to win."

"If you're willing to work from now until the meet, six days, two hours a day . . ."

"The pool is open only five days for training. We can't work six days," Jerri said.

"C'mon. I know—and you know—why you brought me into this. You want to use my pool."

"Aw, Brandon," Mariah cried. "We didn't even think about that." They all joined in denying that they wanted to use his pool.

"Wait, wait," Brandon interrupted. "I thought you girls were a smart bunch. I know I wouldn't ask *me* to coach if I didn't have a pool."

"We happen to think you're a good swimmer. That's why we asked," Cynthia said.

"Okay, okay. I think I can make a decision." He sighed. "I'll do it and I'll plead your case before my parents for use of the pool on Saturdays."

The girls screamed with delight.

"Come on, let's get to work. I can't be here all day," Brandon said.

They decided with Brandon that since the freestyle required more speed, Trina should train for it. Nikki should do the breaststroke because she was strong and had long legs, and Jerri, who danced and had good balance and a good kick, should do the backstroke. That left two categories to be divided between Mariah and Cynthia, diving and the butterfly.

Mariah knew she was the smallest in the group. Cynthia was strong and a good swimmer. Mariah was a good swimmer, too, but she was not quite as strong.

"Maybe I should do diving, Brandon," Mariah suggested.

"Hear this," Brandon said. "She will dive. Diving takes a lot of concentration. I'm not sure about you. For that matter, about any of you." He laughed.

"Aw, Brandon, I bet you think that about all girls," Mariah complained.

"Not *all*. Most." He cracked up.

"And it's not funny." Mariah fumed.

Brandon raised both hands in a truce and said, "Cynthia is tall and has good upper body strength. She's the best for the butterfly. You're good on the trampoline, Mariah. And with your mental strengths, you'll make a great diver, I think."

"Aw, get serious, Brandon," Trina cried.

"Okay. Serious. We should be at the pool six days a week at ten o'clock."

"Too late," Mariah said.

"Yeah," Jerri agreed. "Nine is better."

"Hey, it's vacation time. I have to sleep."

"Aw, Brandon," they all shouted.

"Tell you what. Y'all get there at nine. Exercise, warm up, be ready to really work when I get there at ten. We'll swim until eleven. A deal?"

"A deal!" they agreed as he slapped their palms.

That evening at dinner Lynn and Denise were excited about Kim's party and Mariah had a lot to tell about the swim competition. She wanted Mama to sign the form granting her permission to compete and to make an appointment for her to get a thorough physical exam with the doctor. Then she explained, "The Friendly Five will be the first from our center, ever, to sign up and train for the All-City Swimming and Diving Meet. And you know what? Mr. Lyons is going to let Brandon help coach us."

Her family thought the choices of strokes for Cynthia, Jerri, Nikki, and Trina were good. Then Mariah said, "I'm the diver."

Lynn shouted, "Oh, no!"

"Why did they choose you for that?" Daddy asked.

"Because I'm small and the . . ." She

just couldn't bring herself to say "the smartest," so she said, "and the most mental."

"The most what?" Lynn asked, and laughed.

"The most mental. I'm smart. I can concentrate."

"If you're the best concentrator, then heaven help your team."

"Daddy, make Lynn stop," Mariah cried.

"Lynn . . ."

"Daddy, you know yourself, she thinks off the top of her head, says things without a thought."

Mariah glanced at Denise, who looked with interest from Lynn back to Daddy. Mariah felt humiliated and cried, "Maybe I do say things, but I'm smart and I can learn."

"That's my girl," Daddy said.

"Yeah, that's your girl," Mama said, and smiled. "You're always so pleased when Mariah gets into these different sports. You know, your daddy was hoping you'd be a boy, Mariah."

"Aw, Jean, you don't have to tell Mariah that." Mariah felt that her daddy was a little bit put out with her mama.

"Why not? It's the truth." Mama laughed.

"I think that's normal," Lynn said. "He already had two daughters. I'd think he'd want a son."

"Thank you, Lynn. But tell it all, Jean. What happened after Mariah came?"

Mariah saw her mama soften as she looked at their daddy. "Oh, you came to the hospital to see us sometimes twice a day. And you didn't come to see me, did you, Clark?" She laughed.

"I came to see both of you, but I really went there to see my little girl." He looked at Mariah and smiled. "She was the cutest baby in the whole nursery.

After taking one look at you, Mariah, I didn't want a boy."

"Aw, Daddy, you don't have to explain. I know you love me." Mariah beamed.

"See, Jean, my daughters understand! Now, Mariah, how much time do you have to get ready for the swim meet?"

"We have until the middle of August. Two hours, six times a week. We'll go to Brandon's on Saturdays."

"Brandon's folks agreed to that?" Mama asked.

"Brandon said he'd ask them." Mariah glared at Lynn.

"I was only teasing, Riah. I think you'll do great," Lynn apologized.

"We're in it to win."

"And since no one else over here has ever entered, just to be there will make you a winner," Mama said. "I'll take care of the appointment."

Mariah looked up and caught Denise's

eye. Denise smiled and Mariah felt pleased with herself.

Later she rode with her daddy to take Lynn and Denise to the party. When they dropped them off, Mariah watched them walk to the door: Denise in her short, short skirt and Lynn in her long one. She thought that each looked pretty in her own way and wished she were older so she, too, had been invited.

This had been a busy day. Mariah felt exhausted. She went to take her bath. "What a mess!" she cried. She knew that Lynn had not left wet towels strewn around. Clothes. Fingernail polish and mascara open on the sink. And the tub had not been cleaned. Oh, well, she thought, Denise didn't have time.

Mariah cleaned the bathroom, had a bath, and sank into her bed. Many busy days loomed ahead.

The days rushed by and already it was mid-June.

About halfway between her room and the kitchen, it dawned upon Mariah that she was losing her daddy to Denise. Before Denise came, mornings had been the best time for Mariah: She and her daddy spent quiet time alone as they finished their breakfast, or they talked about any- and everything. As she entered the kitchen, her fear was confirmed. Denise and her daddy were at the table laughing and talking.

Mariah, noticing where Denise sat, felt

a surge of jealous anger. "Do you have to sit in my seat?" She glared at Denise.

"Excuse me," Denise said. "I didn't know you had a seat."

"Well, I always sit there and you know it."

"You can have it. I'm done. Bye, Daddy." Denise kissed their daddy on the forehead and went off to her room.

Mariah's fear and anger stayed, making it difficult for her to find the ease she once felt alone with her daddy. After helping herself to orange juice, she sat next to him and sighed. There was silence.

Finally he spoke. "I didn't know we had special seats in this house."

"Daddy!" she responded as if outraged. "I always sit right here in this chair and you know it."

"Does that make it *yours*?"

What's wrong with him? He's taking up for Denise, she thought, and didn't answer. Again she sighed, feeling more deeply hurt than angry. Controlling her feelings and her voice, she calmly said, "You always sit in *that* chair; Lynn there; Denise in her place; and this is *my* chair, right?"

Her daddy laughed. "As always, Riah, you're right. That's your seat. We'll remember that."

The way he said it made her feel like a five-year-old. "Aw, Daddy!" she shouted.

"Mariah, what's come over you here lately?"

She wanted to scream at him, *What's come over you? It's you, not me.* But again she controlled herself and said, "Nothing."

Just then Lynn walked in. "Morning, Riah."

"Hi," Mariah answered, subdued.

"What's wrong?"

"He's making fun of me," Mariah complained.

26

"No, no, no. I agreed with you." He got up from the table. "Good breakfast, Lynn. Thanks."

"So you liked my pancakes, huh?" Lynn always made breakfast while Mama got ready for work.

"They were delicious. I better run." He pecked Lynn on the cheek and bent to kiss Mariah. She turned away.

"Don't I get a send-off, Riah?"

"I don't feel like that right now."

"Well, okay. You know I'm leaving town in a few days. Try to return to your old self before I go." He left her with Lynn.

"What's wrong with you, girl?" Lynn persisted.

"I get so sick of that Denise. Every morning when I come into the kitchen she's in my chair, grinning at Daddy."

"Aw, Riah. And since when we claim seats?"

"There you go. Just like Daddy."

27

Then she changed her tone and said, invitingly, "Come on, sit down, Lynn."

Lynn sat at the table where she always sat. "Why did you sit there?" Mariah asked.

"I always sit here."

"Yeah, and you know why? Because that's your seat. *Your* seat, Lynn, and that's Denise's seat," she said, pointing to the chair next to Lynn. "And this is mine."

"Aw, girl, aren't you being a bit obstinate?"

"No! Whatever that means."

"It's bending over backward to have your way."

"You and Daddy are bending over backward to please Denise."

"That's kindergarten stuff, Riah. Come fix your breakfast."

"I don't want any breakfast, and I don't want to be in your company."

Mariah stomped back to her room.

She knew she should get ready to go to the center to train, but instead she lay on her bed looking at Sheik Bashara. He stared at her out of dark dreamy eyes under a royal purple turban with a white jewel in the middle of his forehead. That was the poster Denise had given her when she arrived.

Mariah now remembered that day at the airport: how she had been both excited and worried. She looked at the small framed picture of Sheik beside her bed and realized it had been days since she had picked up that small picture and kissed the lips of her favorite rock star. Now she lifted the picture and looked into Sheik's eyes. Suddenly she remembered Denise sitting in her seat at the table. Jealousy flared again. "Oh, Sheik," she whispered. "I still love you, but I just don't have the heart anymore."

She turned out of bed and gathered up the papers from the doctor that said she was in perfect health, fit for the training. Without looking back, she left for her diving lessons.

It was lunchtime when Mariah returned from the center. Lynn and Denise were in the kitchen when Mariah walked in to make herself some lunch. Denise kept her conversation going with Lynn.

"How can you stand it, cooped up in this house? You hardly ever go any place and you never have any company."

Lynn gave a little laugh, as if trying to avoid sounding defensive. "I'm not in the house all the time. And we do have company."

"Yeah, Kim. But where do you go? To the library, the rec center, or the YW. Can't do anything exciting in those places. You can't even talk in the library. Call that fun?"

"Aw, Denise, you know we go to other places. And we can have as much company as we want when Mama or Daddy's home."

"My mama let me have company anytime I wanted. She didn't have to be at home. And there was none of this not being out after midnight. She trusted me. Now you guys, every time you go out that door, you have to say where you're going."

"You mean to say you didn't tell your mama where you were going if you left home? That's ridiculous," Mariah broke in.

"Riah!" Lynn scolded.

"It is. I think it's silly."

"It's different," Lynn interrupted. "All families don't do things the same way."

Mariah pushed her point. "But Denise, what if something happened?"

"What could happen?"

"You could disappear. At least your mama would know where to start looking for you," Mariah said.

"I don't worry about things happening," Denise countered. "Worry about a thing and it will happen."

Mariah sat at the table and began eating. Lynn said nothing. Denise went on, "I gotta get up from here. I'm meeting my friends in a little while."

What friends? Mariah wondered. How and when did she meet anybody?

"Where're you going?" Lynn asked.

"Oh, just out. We hang out around 'Sev.' We ride around in Ron Amory's car. He's real together."

"He looks too old to me," Mariah said. "He has to be twenty, at least."

"So. I'm sixteen."

"How'd you meet him?" Lynn wanted to know.

"Through some people I met at Kim's."

"Did you tell Daddy you were going out?" Lynn asked.

"He didn't ask; I didn't tell. And he

32

doesn't have to know." She got up, pushed in her chair, and started from the room.

"Hey," Mariah called, "it's your turn to do dishes, you know."

"Yeah, I know. I got all day to do dishes. That's the problem in this house: Things always got to be just so. You worry too much." As Denise rushed from the kitchen she called to them, "Chill out!"

Lynn gathered dishes and prepared to prewash them. "Why do you always flunky for her?" Mariah complained. "Let her do her own work."

"Give her a chance, Riah. She has to get used to us and the way we do things."

"She doesn't do anything. Her way, or our way. She leaves the bathroom a mess all the time, and you've seen her room. It's a mess, too. And she's hardly ever out of it now."

"Ah! Listen who's talking about a messy room." Lynn laughed.

"My room is not messy. I got a lot of stuff, yes. But it's all in place and my clothes are sure in my closet. My bed's made, what you bet? Besides I don't walk around here like I'm angry all day."

"Give her time. The way we give you time." Lynn went on rinsing the dishes.

Mariah changed to another subject. "This swimming is doing my hair in, Lynn."

"Why don't you let me braid it in cornrows?"

"No way. I'm not ready to give up my perm, yet. You know what? Maybe Denise is lonely. We ought to give a party. Your birthday is coming up, Lynn. Why don't you have a birthday party?"

"Not me. I don't want a party."

"You know you're weird, Lynn. Break down and have some fun."

"Let's make a deal. When you stop blurting things out and start concentrating, I'll start having fun."

"Wow! Girl, you *are* weird."

Mariah's house was full of hustle and bustle. Everyone was rushing to and fro getting ready for the Juneteenth celebration. On this day every year Mariah's family joined with other families to celebrate the emancipation of African Americans in 1863. Most people celebrated on January first, but in Texas, where Mariah's daddy was born, and in Louisiana, where her mama came from, the Emancipation Proclamation had come six months later, on June 19.

Each year their family went to a different family's backyard or to the park.

Mariah was especially excited today because they were going to Brandon's. She would get a chance to show how well she was doing with her diving in Brandon's pool.

"I'm making the potato salad," she shouted to Lynn, who was outside cutting flowers to decorate the huge table that would be set in Brandon's backyard. Mama had made sweet potato pies, Daddy was almost finished slicing a turkey he had smoked, and Lynn had the vegetables all ready for her contribution: a big garden salad.

Mariah busied herself peeling and chopping potatoes. Lynn came in with the flowers and whispered to Mariah, "Maybe Denise would like to fix a bouquet as her contribution. Go ask her."

"Not me. She's acting funny, and I don't know why." Mariah recalled how Denise recently seemed to be so unhappy. They had all gone shopping the day before with Mama. Denise hadn't wanted to go, but she consented when they all insisted that they didn't want to go without her. Now Mariah wished they hadn't insisted, for the trip had not been fun because of the way Denise had behaved.

Lynn bought a new bathing suit and Mama wanted Denise to get one, too.

"I don't need a bathing suit," Denise said, and walked away to look at a pair of shorts.

"Would you like those?" Mama asked.

"No. I don't want anything." Denise shrugged and walked away. She stayed to herself and didn't say anything to anyone during the whole shopping trip.

When they got home Denise went to her room. When she didn't come out for dinner, Daddy said, "She'll get over whatever it is that's bothering her." But this morning she was still in her room while everybody else was getting ready for the celebration.

Mariah continued to prepare her potatoes. "Let Daddy ask her," she suggested.

"I'll do it," Lynn volunteered.

Pretty soon Lynn returned to the kitchen. "Denise refuses," she said.

"Refuses what?" Daddy wanted to know.

"We thought she might like to do the flowers for the table," Lynn said, and began doing the bouquet.

"Leave them, Lynn. She'll do them." Daddy went to Denise's room.

Uh-huh. I hope he tells her to get her act together, Mariah thought. Why is she acting this way?

Before long Denise came out of her room and started working with the flowers. Mariah knew she was not happy; Denise wouldn't meet her eyes.

When Mariah's potatoes were cooked they didn't seem right to her. "Lynn, come here. These don't look right."

"Riah, what did you do to them?" Lynn asked, surprised.

"I cooked them."

"These look like they're for soup, not salad. Oh, Riah, you never should've chopped them like this. You can't use those."

"Why can't I use them?"

"They won't work—too mushy. Wash more potatoes and boil them whole in their skins."

"And they'll never get done on time, Lynn."

"Cut them into quarters, but leave the skin on. You want them not only to taste good, but to have some of the nutrients left."

"Oh, forget nutrients. People at parties don't think about that. They rave

41

about stuff that looks and tastes good. I'm for raves, what you bet?"

"Oh, my daughters," Mama said as she came into the kitchen. "Denise, did you ever hear so much fuss?"

"No, never." Denise spoke matter-of-factly, as if she didn't want to be involved.

"I like what you're doing with those flowers." Mama praised Denise's efforts.

Mariah looked at Denise and the bouquet. The arrangement was unusually pretty. Denise smiled and said, "I always liked working with flowers."

Finally Mariah's potatoes were cooked. While they cooled, she put eggs on to boil and chopped celery, green onions, pickles, both dill and sweet, pimentoes, black olives, and sprigs of parsley. When the eggs were done she peeled them and got them ready for slicing. Then she mixed the chopped cool potatoes with mayonnaise and stirred in the other ingredients.

Lynn whispered to her, "Add a little mustard and see what happens."

"It better be good, Lynn."

Mariah was surprised at the summery color and the spicy, tangy taste. She spooned the salad into a pretty glass bowl. On top she placed circles of deep yellow and white eggs with a bit of black olive in the center of each circle. Her salad was as beautiful as it was tasty.

With the food all packed in a cooler, around one o'clock, they were all ready to go. All except Denise.

"Don't forget your bathing suit, Denise," Mama called.

They waited, with Mariah becoming anxious. They were late. Twenty-five minutes later, Daddy, his patience exhausted, called to Denise, "Come on, this minute."

Denise joined them with a two-piece swim suit in her hand. That looks like it was made for a doll, Mariah thought. She looked at her daddy, thinking, that's too skimpy for him.

"Denise, don't you have another swim suit?" he asked.

"This one is all right." There was an undertone of anger in Denise's voice.

"Not for my daughter it isn't."

"Then I won't go," Denise countered.

"Yes, you're going even if you don't swim." Daddy was firm.

"We can run and get her one right quick," Mama suggested.

Mariah let out a deep sigh. Now we're really gonna be late. She knew she didn't have a decent suit yesterday, Mariah said to herself. "Can't you drop us off, Daddy, and then take her to get a suit?"

"Won't take long," Mama said. "We'll all go together."

They went from place to place. Denise

tried on every swim suit in her size and nothing pleased her. Finally it was almost three-thirty. Mariah, completely frustrated, cried, "Why can't you make up your mind? We're gonna be *too* late. You're spoiling the whole thing."

"Riah!" Lynn cried.

"Yeah, just shut up!" Denise said seethingly. "I don't have to go, you know."

"And you know who doesn't care if you don't go? I don't. I just wish you'd never come here in the first place," Mariah said.

"Both of you, that's enough," their daddy erupted. "I'm surprised. I am also ashamed."

Mariah felt like she wanted to die. She had gone too far. Why had she said that? Her daddy was ashamed of her. That was the last thing she wanted. She ran from the store back to the car.

When they finally arrived at Brandon's, Mariah felt so upset she didn't want to go into the backyard.

"Get your potato salad and come on, Mariah," her daddy demanded.

Members of the Friendly Five were all there and rushed to meet her.

"What kept you so long?" Cynthia asked. Then she turned to her little sister and said, annoyed, "Tamu, go find your own friends. You don't have to stick around me all the time. Go!"

The others continued their involvement with Mariah, "We thought you weren't coming," Trina said.

"Don't we always come?" Mariah answered with a question and went to put her dish on the long table.

"What's wrong with you, Mariah?" Brandon wanted to know.

"Nothing!" Mariah answered angrily.

"Leave her alone. She's acting odd," Trina complained. She turned to

Mariah. "We haven't done anything to you."

"It's Denise. She made us late, and I don't want to talk about it."

"Sisters!" Jerri cried.

"Heavens, do I know about them!" Cynthia said. "Come, put on your swim suit, Mariah."

Nikki and Trina linked their arms around Mariah's shoulders and Mariah felt a little better.

There were lots of games, circle-dancing, and storytelling. Brandon, of course, had to tell his jokes. Mariah didn't think he was very funny. But in the circle dance she forgot she was un-happy. She was too busy thinking about how to create a new dance step right on the spot to outdo the person she had to replace in the middle of the circle. She hoped it wouldn't be Jerri or her daddy. They were both great creative dancers.

Mariah swam, but she refused to dive. She couldn't really concentrate. She was still too worried about her daddy's outburst.

When they got home the quiet that settled made her feel that they were all waiting for her to apologize for what she had said. She was restless, guilty, but felt she had been provoked. Without saying anything, she went to her room.

She lay on her bed fully clothed, thinking about Denise. Why had she come, anyway? The way Denise talked she had been happy with her mother, who let her go out anytime she liked and stay out as long as she wanted. Never asked her to clean her room or help in the kitchen. Why did she come? Mariah wondered.

Then she suddenly remembered that tomorrow her daddy would be leaving. This time his job would take him to Missouri, Oklahoma, and Kansas to sell medical supplies. He would be gone for five days.

She didn't want him to leave angry with her. She had to talk to him. When she knocked on her parents' bedroom door, she called, "Can I come in?"

"Sure, come on," Mama answered.

Mariah entered the room pleading, "Daddy, don't be mad. I'm sorry. I didn't mean to say all of that and hurt you."

"Mariah, you too often say things that hurt. You're gonna have to watch yourself," Daddy said.

"I'm sorry and I apologize. I'll apologize to Denise, too."

"I'm not upset at you. Remember that. I'm upset about the way you seem not to realize how other people feel. You must be more thoughtful. Come now and let me give you a hug." He held her and Mariah felt the load lift from her chest.

"Sleep well," Mama said as Mariah gave her a kiss.

Mariah stood before Denise's door reluctant to go in, but she had promised. When she said to Denise that she was sorry and apologized, all Denise said was, "Okay."

In her bed Mariah tossed and turned. She knew that it was wrong for Denise to make them late the way she had done. And now Mariah wished she had told her so. But why hadn't Daddy told her? Suddenly she felt sorry for herself.

Mariah did not see her daddy off at the airport. When his plane left she was hard at work trying to perfect the optional dives she had chosen to complete her program of events. Her basic program was five required dives: forward, back, reverse, inward, and a forward one-half-twist. Mr. Lyons and Brandon helped her choose the five optional ones.

"If you can perfect the forward two somersaults, a back somi, a reverse somi, an inward somi, and a back one-half-twist, you could possibly get enough points to win," Mr. Lyons said.

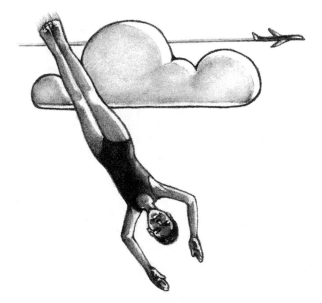

"Yeah, that's good. You'll score high with those dives," Brandon said.

Brandon hammered away at the importance of confidence, strength, personality, and poise. "All eyes will be on you, Mariah. You've gotta look like you know what you're doing and make people think that nobody else can do what you're doing better."

"Work for a few more minutes on the trampoline," Mr. Lyons said. "Test your height. See just how high you can go and do a somersault off into the pit."

Mariah liked the dry land pit, a large sack of foam rubber that was movable. It was soft and safe. She could leap, twist, and somersault onto it without fear of hurting herself.

"Today, we'll practice with the safety belt," Mr. Lyons said.

"Oh, do we have to?" Mariah complained.

"Always when you're doing double somersaults and twists. But first," Mr. Lyons said, "we will work on improving your takeoff over in the pit." He held up a long stick about three feet from the end of the big bag of foam rubber. Mariah, with her eyes on the stick, strained to reach it with both hands.

"Keep your eyes on the stick and your hands," Brandon shouted to her. "This

53

will help you learn not to look at the water as you spring from the board."

"And Mariah," Mr. Lyons said, "make sure you always land in balance and the same distance from the diving board on each dive."

"Reach, stretch out, and keep your eyes on that stick," Brandon called to her.

Again and again she stretched and leaped, sometimes landing on her stomach or on her back without any pain. She liked the pit. It saved time. There was no climbing in and out of the pool on each try.

She was beginning to understand why she had to work so hard on the trampoline and in the pit. Her coordination, balance, power, and a sense of where her body was and how it moved were growing each day.

Now she was tired, but she did not complain as Mr. Lyons hooked on the safety belt for the high somersaults and twists.

Later that morning, she worked with Brandon and Cynthia under Mr. Lyons's supervision. They were now the only ones in the pool. Cynthia was by the diving board waiting to do what Brandon called "troubling the water," making ripples that helped Mariah see where the water level was.

"Concentrate, Mariah. Press down hard on the board to get the lift you need to do those somersaults. Come on. Use your arms to get that lift," Brandon demanded.

"But I've done this again and again. I'm ready to dive."

"You're ready when I say you're ready," Brandon shouted. "Begin!"

Mariah placed her hands on her hips and stomped her foot, but she did as she was told, again and again. Finally Brandon called, "Splash off, Cynthia."

Mariah, standing very still, assumed her starting position and concentrated. She took three steps, tucked for the somersaults, and entered with a splash that looked like a geyser. Terribly disappointed, she cried, "I'll never put all of that together."

"But you will," Brandon said with determination. "You're smart. Your approach is great with your three steps each the same distance. Now concentrate, and right at entry, stretch, point your toes, and cut that water smoothly."

She left the pool feeling that she was trying to do too much with the program she had agreed upon. Maybe she should just give it all up. "But I can do it," she said hitting her palm with her fist.

After all that hard work, her stomach told her it was lunchtime. She hurried home. "I'm here," she called out as she entered the house. There was no answer. Hearing voices from Denise's room, she rushed there thinking that Lynn must be with Denise. She knocked. There was silence.

Finally Denise said, "Yes?"

"What y'all doing?" Mariah walked in.

Denise was with Tracy. They were drinking beer. At first Mariah was so surprised she didn't know what to say. Then she apologized. "I'm sorry, I thought it was Lynn talking to you."

"Now that you've intruded," Denise said, and turned to her friend. "This is Mariah, a part of my *second* family." She laughed.

After that introduction Mariah felt angry and wanted to tell Denise that she was breaking a hard and fast rule. But she thought about what her daddy had said about hurting people and instead said, "I'm glad to see you, Tracy," before she walked out.

Where was Lynn? Mariah wondered. And why did she let Denise do something like that? Surely Lynn knew better. Mariah was so upset she no longer felt hungry.

Before too long she heard Lynn at the front door. She rushed to meet her whispering excitedly, "Where have you been? Denise has company in her room."

"Company?"

"Not so loud," Mariah went on whispering. "She's got that girl, Tracy, in her room. You gonna call Mama?"

"No. Mama won't have to know if she'll leave." Lynn spoke as if she were confident that she could handle it. "Listen, don't you say a word. Let me do it."

Mariah followed Lynn to Denise's room. "Nisy," Lynn called to Denise. "Can I come in?"

"Sure. Come on in."

"Hi, Tracy," Lynn said. Then she went right to the point. "I'm so sorry you've come when Mama isn't here.

We're not allowed to have company when she or Daddy is not home."

"*You're* not allowed to have company."

"No, Denise, *we're* not. So will you please ask your friend to come back later when Mama's home?"

"I'll go," Tracy said. "No big deal. Denise, come with me. Just for a little while." She drank all the beer from the can and placed the can on Denise's dressing table.

"I'd better not. I gotta get something straight here. And do me a favor, Tracy. Take these." She handed Tracy the beer cans.

As Denise let her friend out, Mariah felt worried. "Don't you think you should call Mama?"

"No. Not yet, anyway."

"Lynn," Denise called. "Is that my room, or isn't it?"

"It's your room," Lynn answered quietly.

"Then why can't I have my friends in my room?"

"Because your room is in this house," Mariah said.

"I'm talking to Lynn."

Mariah glared at Denise, but said nothing more.

"Because Mama and Daddy don't want us to be responsible for anyone but ourselves when we are here alone. It's as simple as that." Lynn remained calm.

"That makes absolutely no sense."

"I trust their judgement," Lynn said, and went off to her room.

Mariah wondered if a storm would break when Mama came home.

That evening at dinner, Denise joined in the conversation and acted as if nothing had happened.

"How was the day?" Mama asked.

Mariah waited for that answer. She looked at Lynn. For a moment her heart beat faster. Would Lynn tell?

"It was good for me. I saw two books today, Mama, I'd like to buy."

Mariah breathed a sigh of relief, and rattled off about her difficulties with Brandon at the pool.

When everyone was in bed, Mariah went to Lynn's room. She squeezed into Lynn's narrow bed. "You were *good* today, Lynn. But I thought you were going to tell Mama."

"Tracy left and it all turned out okay."

"Yeah. I wish I were like you, Lynn. But I will be. You just watch."

Mariah felt that she spent as much time imagining herself on the diving board going through the dives as she actually spent diving at the pool. Every morning when she woke up, instead of kissing the Sheik, she lay still, her mind empty of everything except the springboard. She saw herself making the approach, springing up into the air with a high hurdle, and entering the water smoothly, with no splash.

"I can do it," she said aloud to the room, then turned out of bed to start a new day of training.

She looked at her hair and realized that the chlorine in the pool was ruining her perm. Even though she washed her hair daily and put on conditioner, the way her hair looked and felt did not please her. She would ask Mama for a new perm.

Mama was just about ready to go to work when Mariah went to Mama's room.

"Oh, Mama," Mariah said, "you got a new lipstick."

"You like it?"

"Yeah. Can I have your old one?"

"Not yet."

"Aw, Mama. I'm old enough."

"Well, all right, but just in the house, now."

"Can I get my hair done?"

"I'm not paying for your hair with you in that pool every day."

"But I can't go out looking like this, Mama."

"Let Lynn braid it."

"No way. Mama, please. Don't make me suffer."

"Go on, girl. Get out of here," Mama teased.

"It's time you get a feel of the big pool," Mr. Lyons said when the girls arrived at the center that morning. We're going down to the city pool today."

"Maybe you'll see some of your competitors," Brandon suggested.

Mariah, excited about the excursion, wondered what it would be like. She had seen the city pool but had not swum in it. Mariah's excitement stayed as they arrived and went to find the locker room.

Loud shrieks of laughter and the slamming of locker doors greeted Mariah and her team. A noisy crowd of girls, ages six to fourteen, were already there. Mariah and her friends entered. Suddenly there was quiet. Mariah noticed a group of girls near the entrance who appeared to be a team. A tall, fair-haired girl with them said to others in the group, "Get your things! Here, put our stuff over in this corner and, Jenna, you watch it until we find our lockers."

What are they afraid of? Mariah wondered. She looked at members of the Friendly Five and knew that they, too, sensed something was wrong.

"Did you hear that?" Trina asked. "Watch *her* stuff."

"Ignore it," Mariah demanded.

"Yeah, forget her," Jerri agreed. "She just wants to make a scene."

Mariah and her teammates quietly took their time but were out of the locker room and into the water before the girl who had suggested putting away belongings came to the pool with her friends.

"Oh, they swim," the same girl said.

"I thought they were here to clean the pool."

"Stupid heifer, I'm gonna get her straight," Trina said, climbing out of the water.

Mariah pulled her back and splashed water all over as the others gathered around to keep Trina enclosed. Trina went under and came up sputtering. "That kinda talk makes me mad."

"Makes us all mad," Cynthia fumed. "She doesn't know she'll get bum rushed."

"No-oo," Mariah said. "Let's *show* her what we do in a pool. We can outswim them, what you bet." She tried to pretend that what the girl had said did not bother her, but now she wished they hadn't come across town. Swimming in a bigger pool didn't make that much difference. But why would that girl say something like that? She doesn't even know us. Never saw us before, Mariah thought.

After Brandon had tested the diving board to make sure it was safe for Mariah, he suggested that they begin their work. Mariah moved reluctantly, still feeling angry and insecure, remembering what that girl had said.

"Get a move on," Brandon insisted. "What's bothering you?"

"Nothing!" she answered quickly, harshly. Then, noticing the surprised look on his face, she changed her tone. "Really nothing . . . Oh, I'll tell you." She pointed out the girl and told him what she had said.

"That's Lorobeth Dillon. She was at camp last year."

"Then she's a good diver, huh?"

"Pretty good. But I don't really know her. She never spoke to me. Coach always told her to relax, not to think too much about herself. Don't worry about her."

Just then Lorobeth dove off a board and Mariah worried. She knew that Lorobeth was good enough, and if there were others like her in the competition, then winning would not be easy.

A little later that afternoon when Mariah returned home Lynn was there, but Denise had gone out. Mama came home and still no Denise. They prepared dinner and waited. Mariah told them about the incident in the locker room and at the pool.

"I hope you won't let that bother you," Lynn said.

"It bothers me, but not that much. I'm gonna go on diving and stay in the meet."

"That's a winning spirit, Mariah," Mama said.

They still waited for Denise. Mariah

noticed that Lynn, who was usually calm, now acted highly agitated. Finally Lynn said, "I'll have my dinner, Mama. I must go."

"The library doesn't close until nine and it's light out until eight," Mariah said. "You'll have time."

"I gotta go now," Lynn insisted.

"All right, Lynn, you can go," Mama said.

Mariah waited with her mother. Six-thirty, seven-thirty. Lynn returned but no Denise.

"Did Denise say where she was going?" Mama asked.

"She never says where she's going," Mariah answered.

"I'm concerned," Mama worried.

"How come she has to *always* make us so miserable? Always doing something stupid," Mariah commented.

"Not *always*," Lynn said.

"Lynn, why do you feel you have to

defend Denise?" Mama asked. "Denise is irresponsible."

"I'm not defending her. I'm just trying to get Riah to stop exaggerating. Denise is not *always* making us miserable."

"She tries to be nice to impress Daddy and that's the only time." Then Mariah abruptly changed the subject. "Mama, why don't you make Lynn have a birthday party?"

"How silly, Mariah," Lynn said. "You don't force people to have birthday parties. Anyway, I told you. I don't want a party."

"Maybe next year when you're sixteen, Lynn?" Mama asked.

"Maybe. But I'm not promising."

The clock chimed on the half hour. Ten-thirty. The light above the stove cast their three shadows in the room. They did not talk. Mariah knew that her mama was alarmed when Mama said she should call Daddy.

"Wait awhile, Mama; she'll come," Lynn suggested.

"Maybe you should call the police," Mariah said.

"No. We'd call Daddy first," Lynn countered.

"I just can't imagine this. Where is that girl? Who can she be out with? Does she have friends?"

Mariah, thinking something might have gone wrong, decided that Mama should know what had happened. "Maybe she's out with that Ron Amory and Tracy Woods."

"But how does she know a boy like Ron Amory and when did she get the time to find Tracy?"

There was silence. Mariah did not want to say more. She waited for Lynn to speak, but Lynn said nothing.

"Mariah, why do you think she might be out with Tracy?" Mama asked.

Mariah looked at Lynn. Lynn had her eyes down. "Oh, I don't know." She wanted Lynn to tell what had happened, but Lynn sat as if she knew nothing at all.

"Has she been seeing Tracy?" Mama asked Mariah sharply.

"Tracy was in Denise's room, Mama," Lynn said.

"Why did you let her in?"

"I wasn't here when she came."

"Well, why didn't you call me when you knew, Lynn?"

"Because I handled it. I told her she should come when you were here and she left."

"Why didn't you tell me this before now?"

Lynn looked at her mama. "Because I thought I had done what you would've done and that you'd be pleased that it was taken care of. I didn't think it was necessary to worry you."

"It's not your duty to protect me. I'm responsible for what happens in this house and I depend upon you and Mariah to let me know what is going on."

"Why are you acting like you can't trust me, Mama? I let you know when I think it is necessary. I didn't think that was."

"Now you *know*. I don't want you taking responsibility for Denise's behavior—and especially not for her friends. Next time you call me."

Lynn glared at her mama, then lowered her head. "I will, Mama."

Mariah could not look at Lynn. Had she betrayed her when she knew Lynn had handled getting Tracy out of the house so well? And Denise had been so much nicer at dinner that day, too. Why did Denise have to go and spoil it?

Mariah now thought that maybe she should have kept her mouth shut.

At two o'clock Mama went to the phone to call their daddy. Just then they heard Denise's key in the lock.

"She's here, Mama," Mariah called.

"You don't have to wait up for me," Denise said, as if surprised to see them waiting. She started to her room.

"Just a minute, Denise," Mama said.

Mariah was amazed at Mama's calm.

"Where have you been?" Mama asked.

"Out with my friends."

Mama still remained calm as she reminded Denise of the rules. Then Mama said, "Until your daddy returns, if you go out of this house, I want you to call me to say where you're going and I want you back here by the time I get off from work. Is that clear?"

"You're not my mother. You can't tell me what to do."

"I'm the mother of this house and you are a child in this house. And as long as you remain here you are a child. Now if you feel you can't live with us, I'll call your daddy right now and tell him to come home and settle it."

"Please," Lynn cried. "Don't call Daddy from his work. You'll do what you have to do, won't you, Denise? Just three more days."

Mariah thought Lynn looked so small, defeated, as she waited for Denise to make up her mind.

"I'll wait," Denise said, and left the room.

Mariah put her arm around Lynn's shoulder, but Lynn shrugged it off and went to her room. Mariah wished Mama had called their daddy. Things were falling apart.

While they waited for Daddy's return there was a silence between them that did not mean peace. After dinner Lynn went out. Denise escaped to her room.

"Where are you going, to the library?" Mariah wanted to know.

"None of your business," Lynn answered quickly.

Lynn remained aloof, and Mariah knew she was not angry but hurt. Mariah felt that Denise had betrayed Lynn. Then, too, she felt guilty for not having given Lynn the chance to speak first.

But would Lynn have spoken? It was a crisis, Mariah told herself. Mama had to know.

Still feeling upset with Lynn, Mariah went to her room. She looked around, feeling Sheik in her heart, but not in her mind. She tried to clear her thoughts so she could imagine herself doing the dives, visualizing the approach, the lift, the flight, and her smooth entry into the water. In these troubled days, she could not always bring the springboard into focus. What Daddy would say and do about Denise filled her thoughts. Would he send her back? The most pressing question was, Why had she come?

One evening when Lynn went out she looked so sad that Mariah became worried.

A few minutes later, Mariah called to her mama, "I'm going to the library."

She'd gotten the idea that she would sit with Lynn and they then could walk home together.

When Mariah arrived, Lynn was not at the library. Mariah went all over. She finally asked the librarian, who knew Lynn.

"Oh, Lynn hasn't been in for a while. I've missed her. Thought maybe your family was on vacation."

Mariah walked home feeling worried. Where was Lynn going each evening? Was she, like Denise, seeing friends who she didn't want to bring home? Was Lynn riding around in cars? Not Lynn, she thought.

It had been a hot day and it still had not cooled after sundown. Mariah decided to make some lemonade. She invited Denise to have some, but Denise refused. So Mariah and Mama were sitting around the table having the cold lemonade with cookies when Lynn walked in with her arms full of books. Mariah knew that Lynn had stopped at the last minute and collected them. What was Lynn up to?

The next day Lynn was not in the library. Mariah became alarmed. She should tell Mama, she thought. But then, maybe she should confront Lynn first.

When Mariah told Lynn that she knew Lynn was not going to the library, Lynn said, "I never said I was going to the library. You assumed that."

"Then where do you go?"

"I'm not going to tell you."

"Are you seeing some boy, Lynn?"

"What? Don't be silly."

"Then what are you doing?"

"Riah, what I am doing is none of your business."

"Yes it is. You're in some kind of trouble. I don't want to tell, but I'm worried."

"Who will you tell?"

"I'll tell Mama."

"Mama knows what I'm doing."

"Then how come you can't tell me?"

"Because I don't want everybody to know. And Riah, whatever you know, *everybody* knows."

"Lynn, I won't tell. Cross my heart, hope to die, stick a needle in my eye." That was the most solemn vow she could make.

"Nothing else crossed? No fingers, no legs?" Lynn laughed.

"Aw, Lynn. I won't tell."

"All right, you can go to see what I'm doing."

"No! Tell me, Lynn."

"I'm not going to tell you. If you want to know I'll show you."

The next day Mariah walked with Lynn toward downtown into a section where the buildings were crummy and creepy-looking to Mariah. People who worked in that area had all gone home and the streets were quiet. Only strange-looking people were about. Mariah didn't feel comfortable.

Finally they came to a large building that needed paint. Some of the windows were broken and some were boarded. Lynn led Mariah inside. Heat and darkness engulfed them. Mariah became frightened. Then she looked at Lynn, who appeared confident that she knew where they were going. Mariah tried to relax. Odors of food cooking made Mariah think of soup. She never liked soup in summer. Soup to her conjured up cold, wet, wintry days.

As her eyes became accustomed to the dark, a long line of people came into view. Old men and women, young men and women with children. Mariah could see that many of them were dirty; some were ragged and some looked sick.

Then Lynn led her into a well-lighted

room that had rows of tables. People moved busily, putting bread, water, and fruit by bowls on the tables. Those workers greeted Lynn warmly and suddenly Mariah knew that Lynn was volunteering at a shelter for the homeless. Lynn told Mariah where to wait, and got busy filling the bowls with soup.

The long line moved into the room. Lynn, along with other workers, laughed and talked with the people as they entered. Mariah just watched. A little girl ran up to Lynn and hugged Lynn around the legs. Lynn hugged the child back. How can you, Lynn? Mariah said to herself. That little girl is so dirty.

Mariah felt an urge to help serve the food, but she was afraid to get too close to those people. She had seen one or two, alone, on the streets, but she had never seen so many of them together. There were so many children. Some of them ate very slowly, as if they had lost the desire for food, while others wolfed their food as if they were starving.

As she walked home with Lynn later that evening, Mariah had a feeling that she could not define. It was like she had burst in on somebody without knocking. Finally she asked, "How do you do it, Lynn?"

"Do what?"

"Stand those people?"

"Riah! Like I get along with all people."

"But those people are different."

"Yeah. But they are still human."

"How come they don't go to their families?"

"Many of these people don't have families. Members of families don't all like one another, you know. Some of these people are ill. Their families are afraid of them, and can't help them. Those younger people can't find jobs that pay enough to get food and houses for their children."

"That's hard to believe, Lynn."

"Believe it, Mariah."

"You're not scared to be around those people?"

"Am I scared to be around you?" Lynn laughed. "No, I'm not. I'd be more afraid if I were afraid."

At home Mariah could not get those people out of her mind. What did Lynn mean, she'd be more afraid? Maybe something's wrong with me, she thought. But I don't think I can go there. Mariah wished she could be like Lynn. Then she thought, She's so weird.

Suddenly Mariah had an idea. Lynn deserved a birthday party. She would give her one. A surprise. The surprise of Lynn's life. Maybe Denise would help. But maybe Denise would not even be there after Daddy came home.

There was no time at all now for Sheik Bashara. When Mariah was not at the pool or imagining her dives or watching films of famous divers, she worked on building her leg and stomach muscles, both very important to her smooth take-off and entry into the water. Hitting the water was hard on her body. She had to remain strong to keep balance and control. Every morning at the pool before Brandon came, she did sit-ups and leg stretching.

Each day brought Mariah closer to more perfect dives. Her movements were getting more rhythmical, timed and balanced from the moment she began her approach to the time she entered the water. Along with her natural force she moved in tune with the spring of the board to give herself the maximum lift. She knew now that she could concentrate.

She was eager to improve. The Friendly Five were a working team: each girl on her own and all of them together. They were gaining strength and speed and lived for the words of praise from Mr. Lyons and Brandon that were few and far between. Mariah had come to believe that Brandon knew only three words: *Do it again.* Working hard together, the Friendly Five were becoming even closer friends, knowing that they must win.

That day Mariah left Nikki and Jerri and turned onto the street that would take her home. Suddenly she remembered her daddy was coming back late that night. With her mind so full of diving, she had almost forgotten. The rules of their house had to be restated to Denise. How would Daddy do it? she wondered. And how would Denise react?

They had finished dinner. Lynn had gone to the shelter, Denise was in her room, and Mama was beating Mariah badly at a game of Scrabble.

"Mariah, that's not a word," Mama complained.

"*Pya*, that is too a word." Mariah was ready to argue even though she was not sure.

"Never heard that word before. Get the dictionary," Mama suggested.

"Aw, Mama, I never do that to you. Take my word for it."

"No, no. Look it up."

Mariah reluctantly got the dictionary and gave it to her mother. She was about

to admit it was not a word when Mama
said, "Well, it is a word! Mariah, what
do you know about Burmese money?"

Mariah was stunned. She had been
guessing. "Of course I knew what it
meant, but I wasn't gonna tell." She was
so pleased to have gotten those points
that she stopped playing. "Mama," she
said, "let's give Lynn a surprise birthday
party."

"Why give a party when the honored

guest might not come? You heard Lynn say she didn't want a party."

"She won't know. You'll bring her. And when she sees it's a party for her friends at the shelter, she'll be glad."

"How'd you know about the shelter?"

"Lynn took me there."

"You're going to invite all those people?"

"Oh, Mama, no! We'll have Lynn's real friends, like Kim. The only way they can get into this party is to bring cans of food and clothes for the shelter. And the clothes must be something that they themselves would wear. No worn-out things."

"Oh, Riah, you're so clever. That kind of party is a great idea!"

"Don't tell Lynn."

"But how are you going to have a party and get ready for the meet, too?"

"I'll get my friends to help. Too bad Lynn's birthday is not after the meet.

But we'll have a great party, what you bet."

Soon after Lynn came home, their daddy arrived. They made a great fuss. Mariah felt that Denise must hear them and know that Daddy was home, but she did not come to greet him.

He settled down into his chair and finally asked, "Where's Denise?"

Mama explained what had happened. Mariah sensed the uneasiness she had known since the day Denise had brought Tracy into her room. As she listened, she saw the hurt look on her daddy's face.

When Daddy went to Denise's room and didn't return immediately, Mariah became even more worried. What was Denise telling him? Finally he and Denise came into the room. Daddy said, "Now we'll start from the beginning and see if we can know all that actually happened."

"I told you what happened," Denise said.

Mariah smiled within. Denise didn't know that Daddy always heard each side and then brought everybody together to hear all sides. It turned out that Denise had told that she had let Tracy into her room, but she had not said she was out late. When the whole story had been told, Daddy said, "Now Denise, you'll have to live within the rules. You're a member of this family."

"They don't treat me like a member of this family. I don't think Jean even likes me," Denise complained.

"But I do like you, Denise," Mama said. "I must admit that at first I was not happy with the idea of your coming, simply because I thought you might not be happy with us and cause a lot of problems. But once your daddy and I agreed you had to come, I felt then, and still feel, that we can solve our problems as a family."

Uh-huh, Mariah said to herself. We thought she was jealous of Denise's mother, when all along she was afraid of what might happen if Denise came.

"But what about Mariah?" Denise asked. "You all heard her say she wished I had never come."

"After you had made us all late. You were not considerate of us at all," Daddy countered.

"And I apologized to you," Mariah said.

"Denise, you never did to us," Lynn said.

"I don't want to be here!" Denise cried.

"Where do you want to be?" Daddy asked.

"I can go back to my mama."

"That doesn't answer my question.

Where do you want to be? Where will you be happy?"

"Where somebody cares about me. Lets me make my own decisions about what I want to do. Not telling me when and where I can go all the time."

"Denise," Daddy said, "we care about you. But none of us can do what we want to do when we want to do it. We are a family, a unit. We have to have some rules and solve our problems together."

"I can go home to my mother," Denise insisted.

"Will your mother have you back?" Daddy asked.

"I don't know. She made me leave. We weren't getting along when I left."

So that's why she came, Mariah thought in a rush. Her mother doesn't want her. What is it like to have your mother say she doesn't want you? How does it feel? Mariah looked at Lynn. Their eyes caught. Lynn lowered hers first. Mariah suddenly felt sorry for Denise. Maybe that's why Denise was angry at everyone.

Denise went on, "I don't see why I have to stay in this house all the time, or say where I'm going."

"We care about you so we want to know where you are and what you are doing. Is that so hard to understand? We love you, Denise, so we need to know you're all right," Daddy said.

Denise sighed, "I don't like this place. There's nothing to do here."

"You haven't been here long enough to know what is here," Mama said.

Mariah thought of all the things Denise didn't do around the house, or with them when they did things, and said, "You can learn how to cook." Everybody laughed, including Denise.

"Do you really like your room?" Lynn asked.

"I hate that pink bedspread. Never did like pink."

"I wish you had told us so," Mama said.

Mariah listened, thinking, We say what we like and don't like and if we say something that is wrong, we apologize and try to remember not to do it again. "Mama, maybe we can take that bedspread back," she suggested.

"I can use it sometimes on my bed," Lynn said.

"I guess we can use it," Mama agreed.

"You mean it?" Denise asked as if surprised.

Suddenly Mariah thought about how everybody had been bending over backward to please Denise and wondered if Lynn, like Mama and Daddy, had known all along that Denise's mother didn't want her. Maybe Denise could learn to trust and care for them if she believed they truly cared for her. She hoped so. They didn't have time for all those problems. She wanted to get on with Lynn's party. "Sure we mean it," Mariah said. "You're our sister."

Mariah felt that her family was almost back to normal. Denise had redone her room and seemed more at ease when they all gathered in the evenings. But sometimes Denise still acted angry for no reason, like on the day Mariah and Lynn asked her to go skating with them and their friends.

"That's kids' stuff," Denise offered as an excuse.

"There're a lot of us going," Lynn countered. "Some older than you."

"Too small-townish."

Mariah, sensing the sarcasm, asked, "You want to be by yourself today?"

"You can say that," Denise answered, and shrugged.

"No, *you* can say it and it would sound much better than what you're telling us now," Mariah said. Even though Denise might be missing her mother and her friends, Mariah felt she didn't have to appear so mean. But Mariah didn't have much time to worry about Denise and her moods. She was too busy training and planning for Lynn's surprise party.

Right then she was waiting for Lynn to leave the house so her friends could come over to help with the plans. Mama had agreed that they could invite fifty people. Mariah badly wanted to ask Denise to help but she was afraid Denise would refuse. Instead she asked each of the Friendly Five members and Brandon to write down names and telephone numbers of people Lynn knew who might come.

As soon as Lynn left Mariah called her friends and in a very short time they were there.

"That's a lot of people," Brandon said. "How're you gonna keep this a surprise?"

"We'll say to them if they tell *anybody* else, they can't come," Mariah said.

"Tell them they're very special and only special people are being invited," Cynthia said.

"That'll stop them from telling," Trina said. "Everybody likes to think they're special, and wants to be around special people."

"Now won't they be surprised when they see all these people?" Brandon asked, and laughed.

"Aw, stop it, Brandon, and let us see

the names on your list," Mariah said.

"Now everybody I have on my list is special. They're like me and Lynn."

"Weird, huh?" Jerri cried.

"Wait just a minute," Mariah cautioned. "You're talking about my sister."

"And your best boyfriend," Trina said.

When Mariah and Brandon exchanged glances, they all shouted, "Admit it, admit it, Mariah."

Mariah felt her scalp tingle and her heart beat faster, along with a sudden shyness that was strange to her. "Sure we're friends, huh, Brandon?" She didn't look at him.

"I like all you guys," Brandon said, more convincingly than Mariah.

"Not the way you like Mariah," Trina insisted.

"Stop it!" Mariah cried. "We've got work to do."

Each list was checked for duplicates. Some names were dropped, others added. "Maybe we should write down the invitation that we will say on the phone," Mariah suggested.

"Yeah, then we'll all say the same thing," Cynthia agreed.

They came up with this invitation:

You and just a special few are invited to a surprise birthday party for Lynn Metcalf, July 28 at 8 P.M. You must keep it a secret. And instead of bringing Lynn a birthday present, please bring two cans of food and a piece of clothing (not worn-out) to be given to St. Martin's Shelter. It's gonna be lots of fun. You just gotta be there to see Lynn's face when we all shout SURPRISE!!! Can you come?

"Love it," Trina said. "And don't forget to write down whether they say yes or no."

We've got a lot to do," Nikki said.

"Yeah, we'll have to make signs like: 'Surprise! Happy Birthday, Lynn' and 'For St. Martin's Shelter for the Homeless' to go on the boxes that will hold the food and clothes," Mariah informed them.

"We need a theme for this party," Jerri suggested. "Like party for the shelter."

"Ugh!" Cynthia groaned.

"Something with caring and sharing in it," Mariah suggested.

"Got it," Brandon said. "Sharing is caring."

"All right!" Mariah agreed.

"Love it," Trina agreed also.

Later, just before Lynn returned, Mariah told her mama and Denise about the plans. "How will you ever get all of that done without Lynn knowing?" Mama asked. "You certainly can't do it all here."

"Maybe we can do it at Brandon's after our workout," Mariah suggested. "Mama, can you call all the parents and ask if we can?"

"I can do that. That's easy," Mama replied.

"You have a lot to do," Denise said. "Maybe I can help."

Mariah was so surprised and pleased, she shouted, "You really want to?"

"Yeah. Where's the party gonna be?"

"In our yard. We'll have to decorate back there."

"That means a lot of work," Denise warned.

"Daddy'll help. Will you really come to Brandon's and help?"

"Will your friends have me?"

"What you bet?" Mariah asked, and grinned.

"Maybe you would like to invite your friends, Denise," Mama suggested.

"Who?"

"Tracy and Ron Amory," Mariah blurted out.

"I don't see them anymore. They wouldn't come here anyway."

Mariah looked at Denise and thought, She doesn't look unhappy about their not coming. Maybe Denise would meet some new people at the party and start all over again. But best of all, Denise was going to help.

Only four days before Lynn's birthday and nine days before the swim meet. Mariah felt there were not enough hours in the day for all she had to do. Lynn's party took time, but the hardest work continued to be getting ready for the meet. Each step she took as she walked down the street was measured to the approach on the springboard. She often thought about Lorobeth and wondered if all this work was worth it. Maybe she could never compete and win.

Besides now having to spend four hours a day swimming, instead of two, she had to spend time on the party. Each afternoon she worked with Brandon, members of the Friendly Five, and Denise at Brandon's house getting everything ready. Denise was more helpful than Mariah had imagined. Today she was going to show the Friendly Five how to make paper flowers to decorate their yard for the party.

Everything seemed under control except Lynn. Mariah felt that Lynn suspected something unusual was going on when Lynn sometimes suggested that Denise do things with her. Whenever Denise begged off, Lynn, sometimes offended, wanted to know just what Denise was up to.

Mariah was grateful that Mama often stepped in and insisted that Lynn do things with, or for, her.

That afternoon when Mariah was leaving for Brandon's she called, "See you later, Denise."

"Where y'all going?" Lynn wanted to know.

Realizing she had made a mistake, Mariah quickly said, "I'm going to Brandon's to swim."

"So where will you see Denise later?"

"At home. Same time I'll see you. When I get back."

As soon as Mariah reached Brandon's she called and asked her mama to please call home and send Lynn on an errand so Denise could more easily join them at Brandon's.

Finally Denise arrived. In Brandon's room they all got busy cutting colorful paper flower petals and clipping thin wire, wrapping it with strips of green paper to make flower stems. Mariah was surprised at how quickly Denise shaped the petals and stems into beautiful flowers. Soon all the girls were turning out flowers while Brandon worked on signs and banners.

"I think Lynn suspects something," Denise said.

"She better not know. This has to be a surprise," Cynthia said.

Just then Brandon's mother rushed to the door. "Hurry, get out to the pool. Lynn is coming."

They all started up. "Not you, Denise," Mariah commanded. "You hide in here."

"Oh, we don't have on our suits," Trina whispered as they all raced through the house.

"Take off your shoes," Mariah demanded. "Sit on the edge of the pool. Splash your feet."

Mariah listened as Brandon's mama talked to detain Lynn, and when Lynn entered the backyard Mariah called out as if surprised, "Lynn, what you doing here?"

"I was on an errand this way and

thought I'd stop to see how you guys are doing with your strokes for the meet. You're not swimming today?"

"I'm letting them rest for a little while," Brandon said. "They'll be at it pretty soon."

"Please, Brandon, give us the day off," Nikki suggested.

"No way. We gotta work. And Lynn, you had better go."

"Let me see them for a little while. Just once," Lynn pleaded.

"No spectators when we work. Rules. Suit up, girls," Brandon ordered.

"Bye, Lynn," they all sang as they marched inside.

When Lynn had gone they rushed back to Brandon's room. "Whew!" Mariah exclaimed. "Brandon, you saved the day."

"Something's up," Trina said.

"Yeah. But who could've told?" Jerri asked.

"I really don't think she knows," Denise said. "I think maybe she suspects something."

"We better hurry and finish all this stuff," Mariah said. "This is getting to be hard on the nerves."

At dinner on the day before her birthday Lynn announced, "I just want to do nothing on my birthday but rest in bed all day."

Oh, no, Mariah thought as she glanced at Mama and then at Denise. Did Lynn know? Was she going to make it impossible for them to pull the party off as a surprise? Lynn really could be a pain.

"Fine," Denise agreed with Lynn. "Mariah and I will make breakfast and serve you in bed."

"You and Riah make breakfast?" Lynn laughed.

"Sure. We can fix fruit and cold cereal, huh, Riah?"

"You can make your specialty, Denise," Mariah suggested.

"She wouldn't want corn muffins for breakfast." Denise laughed. That was the only thing Denise made successfully since she had started to learn to cook.

"Yours are so good, Denise, maybe," Lynn said.

"We'll give you millet cereal for sure," Mariah said, and they all laughed.

Mariah went to bed worried. How would they ever get ready for the party? If only her sister were not so weird!

Early the next morning Mariah and Denise took a tray to Lynn's room, followed by Mama and Daddy. They sang "Happy Birthday" and as they were leaving Lynn to eat alone, Mama asked, "Lynn are you sure you want to stay in bed all day?"

"I'm sure."

"Aw, Lynn . . ."

Mama quickly raised a hand. "Riah, we must honor that."

In the kitchen Mariah argued. "She can't be here. We'll never get things done. Do something, Mama. Take off from work and get her out of here."

"I had planned to take half a day off," Mama said.

"Hey, remember, Lynn said she wanted some books," Denise reminded them.

"She'd never refuse to shop for books," Mariah said. "And take her to lunch and to a movie, Mama."

"What if she won't go?" Denise suggested.

"She will," Mama said. "She'd better."

Mariah joined her friends at the rec center. They all wanted to know what time to come to get ready for the party.

"Might not be a party." Mariah told them about Lynn's decision to stay in bed all day.

"Somebody talked and she's being cool, huh?" Trina suggested.

"She makes me sick even if she is my sister," Mariah fumed.

"We told you. She's weird," Jerri said.

"I can say that, but you can't, okay?"

Mariah returned home just before noon and Lynn was still in her room. "I don't think she's gonna get up," Mariah said to Denise.

Denise responded quickly, "If she wants to act that way, I don't care. There'll be no surprise. We'll have to tell her."

Just then Mama came home. She went to Lynn's room. Mariah heard her say, "Lynn, I know you don't want a celebration, but I took off so you and I can do something."

"I don't want anything special."

"This isn't special. We'll go to the bookstore. How about that?"

"If we go maybe Riah and Denise would like to come, too."

Mariah wanted to shout *No!* but Mama said it for her, "No, no. We said no big thing. Just me and you. Get up and get ready."

As soon as they were out of the house, Mariah rushed to the phone. "Lynn's left the house. The surprise is on."

By three o'clock that afternoon Daddy had picked up all the things from Brandon's and everyone was there ready to work. Brandon's mother and Cynthia's grandmother came to help, too.

Mariah liked the way Denise had mixed and matched the colorful paper that covered the boxes. Only Denise and Lynn would dare mix those colors, she thought. The boxes were amazingly attractive.

Brandon put his handmade signs on the boxes: MEN'S AND BOYS' CLOTHING; WOMEN'S AND GIRLS' CLOTHING; and there was a box with the sign: CLOTHING FOR SMALL CHILDREN. Then he helped Mariah's daddy string the big banners across the yard so that they could not be seen from the street.

"Where's the music?" Brandon asked.

"Oh, I forgot the music," Mariah shouted.

"What's a party without music?" Trina asked.

"Don't worry," Daddy said. "I'll call Brandon's dad. He'll rig it up." Brandon's father supplied equipment for concerts and big parties.

Soon everything was ready. The yard looked festive as people began to arrive. The Friendly Five worked collecting food to put in boxes marked: CANNED GOODS and STAPLES AND DRIED FOODS.

Denise worked with Brandon's mother and Cynthia's grandmother separating clothing and filling boxes.

Mariah looked around. The yard looked like a magic garden with the flowers and colorful boxes, the lights and banners. People stood together talking softly, waiting. Where was Lynn? Mariah worried. Had something happened?

Brandon's father set up the musical equipment and went to help Mariah's daddy get the grill ready for the hot dogs and bring out the tub of ice for the soft drinks. The cake, hot dog buns, chips, and all the relishes were on the table. Why didn't Mama bring Lynn?

Finally, Mariah heard the car in the driveway. She became so excited she could hardly say softly with force, "Quiet, everybody. She's here."

Lynn entered the backyard and they all shouted, *"SURPRISE!"*

Lynn's eyes widened, her mouth opened, she quickly covered it to stifle the sound and then spun around and tried to escape. Mama held her there until she came to herself.

Mariah beamed. She rushed to Lynn and threw her arms around her. "We did it," she cried. Lynn looked stunned, truly surprised. Mariah watched as Lynn looked at the banners: HAPPY BIRTHDAY, LYNN, WE LOVE YOU and SHARING IS CARING. Then Lynn saw the boxes filled with food and clothing for St. Martin's Shelter. Mariah knew she was fighting back tears when she said, "I didn't want a party, but I'm so glad all of you are here. I know my friends at St. Martin's will be happy to know that you care." She looked at Mariah, "Why didn't I think of this? I bet this was your idea, Riah."

"She's guilty!" a member of the Friendly Five shouted.

"And my friends and our sister, Denise, made it happen," Mariah said proudly. "Give them a hand." After everyone applauded, Mariah shouted, "Let's party."

Brandon picked a record, with some help from the Friendly Five. The music and the smell of hot dogs roasting filled the air. Mariah moved about making sure everyone was getting enough to eat and was having a good time.

Soon she had nothing to do. She stood with her friends watching Lynn and all of her friends dancing. No one asked her or the other Friendly Five members to dance.

"Go ask Brandon to come and dance with us," Jerri suggested.

"Not me," they all cried.

"I'll ask him," Mariah volunteered.

She came back without him. "His excuse is that he's playing the music."

"And Lynn's friends all think we're too young," Trina complained.

"We don't need them. Let's dance together, or by ourselves," Mariah said.

Later everyone sang "Happy Birthday" and shared Lynn's birthday cake and ice cream. After that, the crowd stayed on, reluctant to leave.

After midnight, when all the guests were gone, Mariah, still happy, did not even notice how tired she felt. The Friendly Five huddled with Brandon. "Now on to the meet," Mariah cried. With joined hands raised they shouted, "One down and one to go!"

"We did it once," Mariah said, "and we'll do it again."

119

11

The many weeks of hard work, training, and watching films of champion divers had brought Mariah skill and confidence. Her coaches agreed that she was ready to compete with some of the best in the city. Now with only four days before the meet, she practiced her dives in the order she would do them, polishing and perfecting her program.

As Mariah worked with Mr. Lyons, Brandon carefully watched every move, the position of her head, arms, and legs in each dive. In the hands of Mr. Lyons and under the eyes of Brandon, she felt that her program was a winning one.

At home, Lynn and Denise agreed that until the meet was over Mariah should do nothing but concentrate on her diving. They took over all of her chores, even cleaning Mariah's room. Things were working well for Mariah. That is, all except one thing: Mama still refused to let her get her hair done.

Just two days before the meet, Daddy asked, "Well, Riah, do you feel good about your chances of winning?"

"I'd feel much better if I looked better. Mama should let me get my hair done."

"I think you look just fine," Mama said.

"Yeah," Lynn agreed. "You look great. I think you've grown an inch, maybe."

"You're reeking with health," Denise said, and they all laughed.

"But I want to be beautiful. Mama, please let me get a perm."

"After the meet." Mama's tone told Mariah that was the end of the conversation about her hair.

The day before the meet Mariah awoke at her usual time. She lay in bed knowing her routine today, as the day before, included mostly resting and easy workouts. Her body must have a chance to rebuild and repair. She looked around her room and suddenly realized that Sheik Bashara was not looking into her eyes the way she had once thought. Instead he stared into the distance. This can't be, she said to herself. He must care still. Hadn't he kissed her hand? She sighed. Her mind wandered to Brandon, the swimming pool, to that girl Lorobeth. Then she remembered a recent conversation she had had with Brandon.

"Wow, you're a natural," he had said after practice.

"What do you mean?" she asked.

"You're very good."

She was surprised. Could this be Brandon? He never praised. "How do you know?" she blurted out.

"I've seen a lot of divers, and I've never seen anyone do so well so soon. Your moves are so smooth." Then he added, "But I'm sure my coaching has a lot to do with it."

Now she laughed and turned out of bed thinking, That Brandon. He would have to take back his praise. But I like him. He helped a lot.

In front of the mirror she frowned. What would she do with her hair? Reluctantly she admitted that braiding it might solve the problem. She went to find Lynn.

Lynn was in the kitchen. "It's about time," Lynn said as Mariah entered. "You gotta get started on these carbohydrates. Gotta keep up your energy."

"No millet. I'd like some bacon for breakfast."

"No fats twenty-four hours before the meet," Lynn cautioned.

"Aw, Lynn, you're gonna make me lose my identity."

"You may have some oatmeal, toast, a little jam, and a hot lemonade."

"Can you braid my hair today?" Mariah asked.

"So you've come around to that, huh?"

"I don't want it, but braids will be better than this." She pulled at strands of her hair.

"I'll cornrow it. Make you look beautiful." Lynn glanced at her and grinned. "Let's go to my room."

They decided that an "up style" suited Mariah's small face best. "I'll braid up from the nape of your neck toward the front to the top of your head, from the sides up, and from the front back to the top, okay?"

"Fine," Mariah agreed, knowing right away that Lynn had a different touch. Gentler. Not hurried like the hairdresser who did her perm. Not like Mama's touch when she combed hair. Lynn didn't push her head or pull the comb through so that it hurt.

"You know, Lynn, I'd like to be the way you are."

"Do you know how I really am?"

"No. But I think you're, maybe, kind," Mariah waited. "You're quiet. In control."

Lynn did not respond as she went on braiding Mariah's hair. Mariah remained quiet, too. Then Mariah said, "It's like you know how to do and say things and I don't."

"You know how to do a lot of things I wish I could do. I wish I could play volleyball and swim as well as you. But we're different. We do and say things in a different way. And that's good."

Again they were quiet. Suddenly Mariah said, "Tell me, Lynn, how are you?"

"I'm fine." Lynn laughed.

"You know that's not what I mean, Lynn. How do *you* see you, is what I mean."

"Oh, Riah, I don't know. As you say, I'm quiet. I guess. I try to be in control. I try to own myself in a quiet confident way. But I never seem to be what I want to be. I'm always trying."

Lynn, trying, Mariah thought. "But that's what I'm doing, Lynn, *trying*," she said, then she relaxed under Lynn's gentle fingers.

When Lynn finished Mariah rushed to the mirror. All the braids headed toward the top of her head and ended in one braid that was pinned down with a white barrette. "Lynn!" she exclaimed. "It's beautiful. And you know what? It looks like a melon."

"I'm glad you're pleased. That's exactly what I aimed for—the melon look. Of course, your nice round head helped."

"I'm gonna show it to Denise." Mariah ran to Denise's room. "Look, don't you just love my hair?"

Denise looked up. "Looks like a cantaloupe."

"I know," Mariah said enthusiastically. "Pretty, huh?"

"Who wants to go around with a head that looks like a melon?" Denise asked sarcastically.

"Just you wait. When I stand on that diving board you'll see how beautiful I look."

"No, I won't see. I'm not going to the meet."

"You're not going? Don't kid around, Denise. This is important."

"That's what I said and that's what I meant."

Mariah, crushed, ran to tell Lynn. "How can she be so mean?"

"Riah, I don't think she wants to be that way. She's hurting. And she hits out at whoever is close."

"But that's silly, and I know, Lynn, she *tries* to be mean."

"No, she doesn't. She thought her mama might let her come back home. But her mama said no. Now how would you feel if Mama told you she didn't want you in this house?"

"I don't know. I guess I'd just die."

"Well, being mean is easier than dying. So try to understand Denise. She misses her mama *and* her friends. Give her time. Why don't you go back and tell her you won't mind if she doesn't go if she will wish you well and hope you win."

"I can't do that. She's too much."

"Think about it. It's hard to be nice when you're in pain."

"Oh, you know so much, Lynn," Mariah said. She stormed out of Lynn's room and went to her own room, still fuming. Of all the things on her mind: the meet, that Lorobeth, and now Denise. Forget Denise. She just makes everybody miserable. But maybe Lynn was right. She couldn't imagine Mama not loving her. Not wanting her.

She went and knocked on Denise's door. "Can I come in?"

"Come in," Denise called disinterestedly.

Mariah at first didn't know how to say what she had to say. Denise waited, not looking at Mariah, not helping.

Finally Mariah said, "You know, it's all right if you don't come to the meet. But I'll be real unhappy if you don't wish me well and hope I win."

Denise looked up. She seemed to be thinking. Then she said, "Sure I'll wish you well, Riah. I know you'll win. I'm sorry, but I don't want to go anywhere."

"It's okay," Mariah said. She rushed forward and kissed Denise on the cheek, then left, quietly closing Denise's door, glad she had followed Lynn's advice.

That night she went to bed feeling both doubtful and confident. Would everything go well? One little something— a foot out of line, or a break in her rhythm—could mean the difference between a loss and a win. So much can go wrong, she thought. She smiled, thinking of the blue swim suits the team had chosen. Blue like the championship ribbons; and their sweats were yellow, the color of the winning gold. Her team had better win.

Now, as she did every night before she went to sleep, she imagined herself on the diving board doing one dive after another, smoothly entering the water.

Early in the morning, Mariah rode across town with the members of the team, quiet and subdued. She stared out of the window of the van, wondering why she had ever thought she and her friends could win against people who were in swim meets all the time. She and her friends had never swum in a meet. What was it like, she wondered? Would Lorobeth and her friends be there today?

When they arrived they had to stand in line at the registration table. There were so many teams wearing sweats of all colors. Mariah saw Lorobeth with her team dressed in royal purple.

Finally their turn came to register. All the officials smiled warmly and acted as if they had been waiting for them. Mariah and her friends signed the permission forms that had already been signed by their parents and Mr. Lyons.

Later Mariah sat and filled out her diving scoresheet. Brandon and Mr. Lyons did some last-minute coaching with the team during the warm-up. Other teams were getting last minute instructions, too, showing off their best, trying to intimidate. Suddenly she remembered the words "thought they were here to clean the pool." Maybe we shouldn't have come, she thought.

The other Friendly Five members came through the preliminaries, qualifying for the finals in the competition for eleven- and twelve-year-olds. The joy of their staying in the competition helped

Mariah in her diving. She felt at home in the large city pool.

"You're in rare form today," Brandon told her after she had completed her five required dives. "I believe you can walk away from here a winner."

Mariah didn't feel so confident. Besides Lorobeth, there were other good divers. But when all the divers had finished Mariah was among the eight listed in the finals. She had done well, and she and Lorobeth were top scorers, with Lorobeth leading Mariah by two points.

At the end of the preliminaries, the Friendly Five concluded they were in competition with Lorobeth and members of her team only. "If we come out ahead of them, I don't care if we don't beat anybody else," Trina declared.

That evening, for the finals, the grounds around the city pool were filled with families and friends of the swimmers. People brought picnic baskets; the city provided music and the atmosphere was festive. Mariah was disappointed that Denise had not changed her mind, but she was glad that the rest of her family had come. They joined the families and friends of the Friendly Five.

At six o'clock the finals began. Mariah sat with her family to cheer their team. Mariah tried to restrain herself, but she forgot about saving her strength when the medley relay got underway. Jerri, with her fast reflexes, got a good start and moved ahead in the backstroke. At the touch, Mariah cheered as Nikki dove in for the breaststroke. And when Cynthia touched on the butterfly to give Trina a lead in the freestyle, Mariah lost control. They won the four hundred medley relay.

In their age group, they took first in the one hundred free, a second in the one hundred breast, and a third in the one hundred back. Cynthia was just touched out in butterfly for a second.

Then it was Mariah's turn. The officials announced the names of the eight divers, but Mariah was concerned with only two names: hers and Lorobeth's. "Lorobeth Dillon, first diver; Mariah Metcalf, fifth diver."

Mariah racked up scores with the three judges giving her sevens, eights, eights and one-halfs, and even a couple of nines. But Lorobeth's scores were right up there, too. When they had finished their required five dives and the first four optional ones, their scores were tied.

Mariah wished it were all over. If only she had chosen a more difficult program. But then she might be out of the competition: A tough dive not well-executed could be the kiss of death, bringing down the total score. Brandon and Mr. Lyons assured her she had done well and had a good chance to win.

Mariah paced back and forth, swinging her arms, breathing deeply, trying to relax. She heard the announcer call the final round. "Lorobeth Dillon will do a back dive with one somersault in the tuck position, degree of difficulty one point five."

"Oh, no," Mariah said. "That's my dive!"

Mariah's heart sank as she looked at Brandon. Brandon smiled. "Don't worry about that. You're lucky you come second. You have time to really concentrate and see yourself doing your dive."

Mariah didn't want to concentrate. She wanted to see her competitor. Lorobeth had style and grace. She stood tall and straight, motionless as she planned every move. Now, in the final dive, Mariah felt that Lorobeth stood forever before she slowly raised her arms preparing for the back takeoff. Finally, Lorobeth somersaulted backward in a tuck position. She misjudged her timing and straightened her body, opening her dive too soon. She landed on her stomach, and the crowd groaned.

At first Mariah was elated. Then she felt an added tension. She must not open up too soon like Lorobeth did, but she couldn't be too late either. Too late would put her on her back. Her timing had to be just right.

"Mariah Metcalf will now do a back dive with one somersault in the tuck position, degree of difficulty one point five," the official announced.

Mariah stepped up on the board and glanced at the judges. Then she slowly walked to the end of the board, turned around, and carefully balanced herself with her head held high, eyes straight ahead, body erect, and arms straight at her sides. She stood motionless, concentrating on the dive. She waited, feeling the expectant silence. All eyes were on her.

Just before she made her back press she breathed easily, seeing herself making a perfect dive. "For those who are thought only capable of cleaning the pool," she whispered. As she pressed back her arms reached up and she brought her knees to her chest. She felt herself turn. She opened right on time, ripping the dive and entering the water without a splash.

The roar of the crowd pushed through the water in her ears and she knew she had won.

Later, at home, Mariah showed off her trophy. "I know you wished me well, Denise. And your wish came true."

All the family beamed. Lynn said, "Ri-ah, that last dive you made was so right on. For a moment though, I thought you would never move. What were you thinking?"

"I was worried, what you bet?" and she told again what had happened in the locker room and at pool side. "And facing that Lorobeth was really tough. I knew I had to win." She looked at each one in her family, as if to bring them all together and said, "I had to do it for us."

MILDRED PITTS WALTER began writing for young people while she was a teacher in Los Angeles, California. Among her well-honored books are the winner of the 1987 Coretta Scott King Award for Fiction, *Justin and the Best Biscuits in the World,* and the Coretta Scott King Honor Books *Because We Are* and *Trouble's Child.*